XTREME
MYSTERIES

#1 DEEP POWDER, DEEP TROUBLE

Laban Hill

HYPERION PAPERBACK

XTREME MYSTERIES

#1 DEEP POWDER, DEEP TROUBLE

1

"This puppy isn't coming off for the entire week," Jamil Smith cracked to his best friends, Kevin Schultz and Natalie Whittemore, as he waved his snowboard. Together they were riding up the chairlift to the top of Mount Olley, the tallest peak at Hoke Valley Ski Resort.

"I'm making an *A* in science," Kevin added. "This attachment operation should be a snap."

"I can't wait to see you try to hop into the bathroom with a board attached to your feet," Nat said, smirking. Then, after a pause, "On second thought, forget that." She covered her eyes with her thickly insulated mittens.

"Very funny," Jamil cracked.

"This is the only way to begin a whole week off," said Kevin. Half an hour earlier, like prisoners being paroled, they had been released from Hoke Valley Middle School for spring break.

As far as they were concerned, the best thing about living in a Colorado resort town was that there was still plenty of snow on the slopes in March. Spring break meant that they could spend all day—not just all afternoon—snowboarding.

Jamil, Nat, and Kevin had been friends since kindergarten, and they all had one thing in common: They were extreme sports freaks, and they were all wicked competitive. Nat was definitely the best mountain biker, and could even catch air with the best of the BMX bikers. Jamil was the best snowboarder, but that wasn't surprising: his dad was the Hoke Valley Resort manager, and literally lived on the slopes. Kevin was the envy of both Nat and Jamil—he could bike, board, sport-climb, and skateboard with incredible skill.

"Boards up!" announced Kevin. They were approaching the end of the lift ride. Kevin knit his brow as he concentrated on dismounting the chair. He approached everything he did with logic and mathematical precision—even sports.

All three lifted the noses of their boards and leaned forward. As they hit the ramp, they slid down and dragged their free foot to stop.

"You chumps up for the boardercross course?" Kevin asked as he strapped in goofy. "I want to get in some practice before Wednesday's race. My technique on the jumps is weak." The boardercross was just one part of the big carnival that Hoke Valley Ski Resort threw every spring break. The festival lasted the entire week and offered a mix of ski racing, music jams, and parties. This was the first year that Hoke Valley was including snowboarding events in its schedule.

Jamil nodded. He was hip to shredding Freight Train, which was a double black-diamond trail and the site of the boardercross competition. It was his favorite ride.

Nat coughed. The cold air tightened her throat. "Yeah, my jumps need work, too, but I guess you won't be giving me tips, Kev."

Kevin laughed. "You got that right." Nat and Kevin were the most determinedly competitive of the group. Jamil, on the other hand, was too cocky on the slopes to see his friends as real competition.

Jamil puffed out his chest. "Well, Nat, you can try to pick up some style and technique from me—while you eat my powder."

"You might ride regular, but you're totally goofy," Nat said with a smile.

Jamil clutched his chest. "That's cruel." He took a couple of short hops to turn his board downslope. The board slid to the left a little, but Jamil easily controlled it to keep his balance.

"Sick!" Kevin exclaimed. "The powder's rad after last night. That's got to be the last blizzard of the season." The night before, clouds had dumped more than twelve inches of fresh snow on Hoke Valley. Snowboarding nirvana.

"Ready?" Nat asked. She did a deep knee bend and stretched her arms over her head to loosen up.

"Rockin'!" Jamil yelled as he gave Nat a quick shove and headed down the slope.

"Hey!" Nat tipped backward and landed on her butt.

"That's for calling me goofy," Jamil shouted over his shoulder. He hucked a bonk and swayed down the fall line. Kevin fell in behind Jamil, while Nat flopped over on her hands and knees and pushed herself back onto her board.

Surfing the slope, Jamil and Kevin gracefully moved in and out of the long, late-afternoon shadows. As Jamil's board floated from one turn to the next, his body riding and sinking with the rhythm of the turns, Kevin sped past him, spraying snow directly in Jamil's face.

"You're stylin', dude!" Jamil sucked a couple of flakes into his mouth and smiled at Kevin. Kevin rarely wiped out. He rode with a precision and confidence that made him seem much older than thirteen. But Jamil, at twelve, was definitely the favorite in the boardercross because of his economical style.

Nat rode in a tense crouch, trying to make up as much ground as possible between her and her friends. She shifted her weight forward and dug her toeside edge into the powder.

Just ahead, Jamil took air off a mogul. He tried a 180 to fakie, but couldn't stick the landing. He plowed face forward down the slope.

"Nice facial!" Nat laughed as she glided down next to Jamil.

Jamil shook snow out of his blond dreadlocks. "Next

4

time." He shrugged.

Nat started downhill again, but quickly pulled up. Snow sprayed up the legs of her baggy tan snow pants. "Oh, I almost forgot. Definitely thank your dad for putting boarder events in the carnival." Jamil's dad, Ned Smith, was the mountain manager of Hoke Valley Ski Resort. He was not a fan of snowboarding, so it took a lot of smooth talking on Jamil's part to convince his dad to include a boardercross and a big air event among the skiing races.

"I didn't think he'd do it," Jamil replied. "He's such a ski snob, and he's always blaming boarders when anything goes wrong."

"Come on now, don't be so modest," Nat said. "With your awesome powers of persuasion you can almost get anybody to do what you want."

Jamil smiled. "Yes, it's true. Lesser mortals would have caved under the task, but I, with my third degree black belt in verbal sparring, am only energized by such odds." He stood and brushed snow off his blue snow pants. "I just hope everything goes smoothly. I can see him using any excuse possible to never do it again."

"I don't think there'll be a problem," Nat said, "especially since you suggested posting those 'Boarder Rules' signs. I can already see an improvement in shredder etiquette." Nat always looked on the bright side of things.

"Hey! Break up the tea party and let's ride!" Kevin shouted from about two hundred feet below. He had stopped to wait for them, but was now getting impatient.

"Shred it!" Jamil yelled down to Kevin. He tipped his own board downslope and quickly plowed through a recess of deep powder. He carved wide furrows as a huge fan of snow followed his tail. His breath was like a piston pulling and expelling icy air. His legs pumped up and down with each bonk, the bumps barely registering in his upper body. Without a doubt, Jamil was the smoothest rider in the valley.

Up ahead, Kevin carved onto an access trail to cut across to Lolo's Ridge, the site of the big air contest on Tuesday night. Kevin took it straight on and did an awesome tail grab.

Nat followed with a fluid 180 to fakie. Jamil leaned radically toe side, making a tight Eurocarve. His right hand skimmed lightly along the snow and he shot uphill like a bullet. With a quick twist he spun fakie to take Lolo's Ridge backward.

Suddenly, a hand came out of nowhere and gave him a little shove. Jamil pitched forward and did a shoulder roll. His board, still strapped to his feet, flipped high into the air.

Jamil looked up and saw Mitch Richards, a thirteen-year-old classmate, cutting right past him and heading for Lolo's Ridge.

"Too slow!" Mitch yelled back at Jamil. Then he performed an amazing 360 with a tail grab.

At that moment, another spray of snow hit Jamil's face. As he wiped it away he saw Mitch's new friend, Wall Evans, zip past him and off the jump.

"No style!" Wall yelled as he sped by.

Jamil bounced up and went after Mitch and Wall. At the bottom of the slope the two were laughing as they watched Jamil head straight for them.

Mitch was all flash. He was always down with the right board and the lastest swag, emblazoned with the hottest logos. Jamil didn't know much about Wall, other than that he had moved to Hoke Valley recently and immediately hooked up with Mitch.

"That was a total bonehead move, dude," Jamil

shouted at Mitch as he leaned right into his face.

"Bad breath, dude," Mitch replied as he pushed Jamil back. He pulled off his purple striped knit hat and rubbed his short brown hair.

Jamil took a step toward Mitch when Kevin came up behind him and pulled him back.

"Chill," Kevin whispered. "He's a bug."

"On a windshield," Nat added as she stepped between Jamil and Mitch. "With a bad case of hat head!" She pointed to Mitch's hair and laughed.

"My dad wants to ban us because of stunts like that," Jamil said. He walked over to the community bulletin board and ripped off a sheet of paper. He came back and shoved it down Mitch's jacket. "Read this and learn how to ride."

Mitch fished the paper out of his jacket. "Boarder Rules at Hoke Valley Ski Resort," he read aloud. Then he spoofed the rules:

"One. Never board under control.

"Two. Always ignore and run over the skier or rider below you.

"Three. Stop wherever you want.

"Four. When entering a trail, always cut off other skiers or riders.

"Five. Never wear your leash, so your runaway board can be a missile lopping off all heads below.

"Six. Ride wherever you want. Ignore all posted signs.

"Boarders rule!" Mitch crumpled the paper and tossed it in the air. Then he headed for the parking lot.

Jamil froze, mouth agape.

Wall followed Mitch, but turned back and waved. "See you," he mumbled and shrugged.

"Who is that guy?" Nat asked, nodding toward Wall. "He's pretty quiet at school."

"His name's Wall Evans," Jamil said. He pointed to a snowboard boot print in the snow. "And he's got a cool set of treads on his boots." The treads were a design of diamonds encircling arrows that pointed to a shape that looked like a tongue sticking out.

"Yeah, they're called Ragers," Kevin explained. Kevin knew everything about snowboarding equipment. His mom and dad owned Alpine Sports, a winter sports store in town. His dad had been the first African-American on the national ski team twenty years earlier. Like his dad, Kevin loved winter sports. "You can only get them through a catalog. And that makes sense. From what I hear Wall just moved here from the backwoods near Barton Mountain."

"So he hasn't learned what a jerk Mitch is, yet," Jamil added. "But I have to admit, Mitch is going to be tough to beat in the boardercross Wednesday. I don't know if I'm up to it."

"Don't sweat him," Nat said. "You can outride Mitch twenty-four/seven. He's just another knuckledragger."

"Come on, boardheads," Kevin said as he pulled Jamil by the sleeve of his gray-and-brown jacket. "Let's grab a mug o' choc."

"I just hope he doesn't pull a stunt like that during the

carnival," Jamil said. His sunburnt brow furrowed. "If my dad hears of any problems this week, that's the end of boarding at Hoke Valley."

"Mitch is all bark, no bite," Kevin reassured Jamil. They pushed open the doors to the lodge. A blast of warm air melted the ice that had collected on their eyebrows.

Jamil wiped the water out of his eyes. "I hope you're right."

Nat made for the giant hearth, where a large fire roared and skiers gathered to get warm. The lodge was pretty empty since the spring carnival didn't actually start until the next day.

Jamil went into the snack bar's back kitchen and poured hot chocolate for himself and his friends. Since his dad ran the place, he could go anywhere in the resort. When he came out, balancing three mugs, he noticed his dad in an intense conversation with the resort's hotel manager. His dad's large, round face was flushed and angry. His hand chopped the air with force.

As Jamil handed warm mugs to Nat and Kevin, he nodded toward his dad. "I wonder what that's about?"

Nat shrugged. "Must be about the carnival. You said he's been going nuts about it for the last week." She put her feet up on the table in front of the hearth. Snow dripped from her boots into a small puddle in the middle of the newspaper under her feet.

"Hey," Kevin protested, "someone might want to read this." He snagged the paper from under Nat's boots and froze when he saw the headlines. "Uh, Jamil, I don't think your dad's upset about the carnival." He handed the soggy copy of Friday's *Hoke Valley News* to Jamil. A big two-inch headline spanned the entire top of the paper: ROGUE RIDERS RUIN RESORT.

Jamil grabbed the newspaper out of Kevin's hands and began reading. "For the past few months skiers have been tormented by snowboarders on the slopes of Hoke Valley Ski Resort. According to anonymous sources, a group of young snowboarders have been egging each other on to perform more and more dangerous stunts. The result has created unsafe conditions for all who use the slopes. These rogue riders have blatantly ignored Hoke Valley's 'Boarder Rules' posted around the resort, and consciously tried to break them whenever possible. Pauline Pardo, a vacationing skier, expressed annoyance. 'They're always cutting people off.'

"An anonymous resort regular said, 'There has definitely been a rise of snowboarding incidents this season.'

"One young boarder confirmed these details by raising his fist and yelling, 'Boarders rule!'

"Whaaaa?" Jamil gasped. "What nutcase came up with these lies?"

Kevin pointed to the byline of the article, Debbie Windsor.

"Look at this," Nat said as she grabbed the paper from Jamil. "The article also says that it's only a matter of time before someone gets seriously hurt!"

Jamil collapsed onto the couch in front of the hearth.

He pulled the zippers down the legs of his blue snow-pants and let out a loud, deep sigh. "This is exactly what my dad doesn't need with the spring carnival starting tomorrow."

Nat and Kevin brooded beside Jamil. Their eyes followed the flickering flames of the fire as it licked the logs in the hearth.

Finally, Nat reassured Jamil. "It'll blow over."

"No, it won't," Jamil moaned. He slumped into his seat.

"What won't?" Ned Smith asked as he came up behind his son.

Jamil buried his chin in his chest.

Mr. Smith sat in a chair across from his son. "What's up?" He forced a smile.

Nat held up the *Hoke Valley News* and grimaced.

"Oh, you saw that, too," Mr. Smith said as he shook his head in disgust.

"Where'd this reporter get her information?" Kevin asked.

Mr. Smith scowled and rubbed his bearded chin. "I honestly don't know. As far as I can tell, she based her story on an anonymous fax the paper received and a couple of interviews with people on the slopes." He sighed deeply. "I just don't understand why she didn't call me to check her facts." Mr. Smith leaned over and gently slapped his son's knee. "Got to go. I'm swamped with the carnival prep."

Jamil nodded without enthusiasm.

"No matter how you slice it, whenever snowboarders are involved, there's always trouble," Mr. Smith said. "Now I wish I hadn't agreed to add the boardercross and big air events to the carnival." He walked away briskly toward his office.

Jamil grabbed a fistful of his dreadlocks. "We're doomed. I know my dad is just looking for an excuse to bag boarding. Now he's got one!"

"Don't worry," Nat replied. "After the carnival is a success and we show him how cool and popular boarding is, he'll forget all about the article."

"Relax," Kevin said. "We've got a whole week to board and—"

"No school!" Nat finished Kevin's sentence for him. She punched her fist in the air.

Jamil sucked down the last drops of his hot chocolate. "I just wish I knew who would try to mess up Hoke Valley."

"Obviously, a nutcase," Nat said.

"What about Mitch?" Jamil countered. "He's crazy enough."

Kevin shook his head. "Not a chance. He wouldn't do it because it would hurt him, too. Like I said before, he's all bark and no bite."

"I'm not so sure," Jamil protested. "Look at this article again." Jamil pointed to the newspaper. "The anonymous sources say the same thing about the boarder rules that Mitch just said."

Nat nodded. "Also, Mitch said 'Boarders rule' just like

the snowboarder in the article!"

"That's just the kind of joke Mitch would play," Jamil said emphatically.

"It could be a coincidence," Kevin said halfheartedly.

Jamil glanced up at Kevin and stared at him for a few seconds before he started laughing.

"What now?" Kevin asked.

"Oh, it's nothing." Jamil smirked. "It's just your haircut." He paused trying to stifle a laugh. "With your afro shaved close like that, your head looks like a sharpened pencil."

Nat snickered. "Yeah, but at least his head doesn't look like he glued a piece of shag rug salvaged from a garbage can on it."

"Or a Smurf convention," Kevin cracked.

"That's brutal, man." Jamil laughed.

Early Saturday morning, Jamil woke in his usual state—tired. No matter how much sleep he got, he couldn't seem to wake up. He sat up in his bed and rubbed his eyes. He looked around his room and saw his pile of clean clothes in one corner and his dirty ones in another. His mom had given up on trying to get him to fold his clothes and put them in his dresser. She gave up on that around the same time she stopped making him tuck in his shirt and wear a belt.

Jamil pulled on a pair of blue corduroy pants without even undoing the snap or zipper. He liked his clothes large. He slipped on his favorite T-shirt, which had a picture of a doe-eyed girl about to be creamed by a hideous robot, pulled a thick green wool sweater over it, and padded downstairs.

"What up, Mom?" Jamil said as he slid into the kitchen.

"What up, yourself," Katie Smith replied. She was

pouring some orange juice. "Get your boots on. I need you to go to the market for milk. We're out."

"Awwww, Mom," Jamil complained. "Why can't we eat our cereal dry?"

Mrs. Smith raised one eyebrow.

Jamil still protested. "It's cold outside." He pushed back the curtain on the kitchen window.

His mom walked over to the freezer and pulled out frozen waffles. "Now, hurry up."

Once outside, Jamil stepped gingerly down the front stoop. One cool thing about his dad's job was that the family lived in a condo right on the slope.

The gray sky was low and cold this morning. Ten-foot-high banks of snow lined the edges of the street. There was no sidewalk, so Jamil walked on top of the snowbank and imagined himself as an arctic explorer who hadn't seen another soul for weeks. He scanned the horizon for any sign of human life.

"Wow!" Jamil blurted.

He not only spotted human life, he spotted one of the best skiers in the country. Dave Swenson was coming straight down Freight Train with barely a cut.

"He must be going a hundred at least," Jamil gasped. He scrambled over the snowbank and dashed toward the lodge to get a better look.

Up on the wide deck that extended from the second floor of the massive log building, Jamil watched in awe. He'd never seen someone ski like that, except on television.

Mr. Smith came up behind Jamil. "Amazing, huh?"

Mr. Smith had been up since long before dawn, working on the spring carnival.

Jamil could only nod. He didn't want to break the spell of Swenson's skiing.

"You could ski like that," Mr. Smith added, "if you didn't spend all your time snowboarding."

The hairs on the back of Jamil's neck bristled. "Won't you ever let up?"

Mr. Smith had gone to college on a downhill skiing scholarship. Ever since, he had devoted his life to skiing, so when his son took up riding three years earlier, he hadn't really accepted it. Sometimes Jamil felt that his father just wanted him to be a clone of his older brother, Ramon. Ramon was a champion skier and straight-A student. Jamil got along with him, but he was secretly glad that Ramon was away at college so that his dad couldn't compare them as closely.

Mr. Smith agreeing to allow boarding events during the carnival was a major breakthrough. Jamil had hoped this meant that his dad was finally accepting his choices. Boarding was one of the first activities Jamil had ever followed through on. He wished his dad could see that. But now it seemed that just as he was poised for success, his efforts would be trashed by dangerous boarders like Mitch, and by the *Hoke Valley News* article.

"Got to run," Mr. Smith said. He was too preoccupied with the festival to have even registered his son's response. "There's a lot to do if day one is going to go off without a hitch."

Jamil watched his dad lumber back inside the lodge. He kept his eyes on the door long after it had closed, hoping his dad would come out and take back what he just said. But he didn't. Jamil grabbed the railing and squeezed it until his knuckles were white. "Mitch, you're not going to ruin this festival," Jamil said to the wind. He took a deep breath. "Nobody, and I mean nobody, is going to prove my dad right—because he's wrong!"

The sun had finally risen from behind Mount Olley, and it shone brightly in Jamil's face. He stood there and soaked up its warmth until a voice penetrated a corner of his mind.

"Jamil!"

Jamil turned and saw Chip Levin coming across the deck toward him. Chip was the resort's gofer this season. He was putting himself through business school doing odd jobs around the resort and pinch-hitting at the ski school when instructors didn't show up.

Jamil started to smile until he saw Chip's serious expression.

In Chip's hand was a tightly held piece of paper. He handed it to Jamil. It was a copy of the boarder rules covered in red ink. "I found this hanging in front of the office when I came in this morning. Since then, I've seen three other signs ruined."

4

"Oh, no!" Jamil cried. "It's already starting."

"What is?" Chip asked. He shivered in the morning cold and hugged his arms. He hadn't even bothered to put on his jacket.

"This jerk Mitch is out to make my life miserable," Jamil said. He crumpled the paper in disgust. "He thinks he's being cool by doing exactly what he's not supposed to do."

"Yeah, I get the picture," Chip said. "He's not going to follow the rules because they happen to be rules. He hates anyone telling him what to do."

"And that means," Jamil added, "when my dad finds out about his stunts, boarding is history at Hoke Valley." Then, Jamil got an idea. "Chip, can you do me a favor?"

"If it's within my power," Chip answered.

"Please, please, don't tell my dad about this," Jamil said. "If he finds out now, he'll go ballistic."

"No kidding," Chip said. "With all the pressure of

running the carnival, he blows up at least five times a day. I can imagine what he'll do if he finds out about this."

The deck around them was beginning to fill up with skiers and boarders loaded down with equipment. The lifts would start in a few minutes and the first day of the carnival would begin.

At that moment, Jamil was startled by the sight of Mitch coming across the parking lot with Wall. He didn't expect to see Mitch so early in the day. He watched as they carried their snowboards toward the Mount Olley chairlift.

"I'll keep my mouth shut if you replace the markedup signs with some extras I have in the office," Chip suggested.

"It's a deal." Jamil grinned in relief. Then he got serious again. "But first I'm going to take care of Mitch. Boarding at Hoke Valley isn't going to suffer just because of his practical jokes." He started toward Mitch and Wall, but Chip grabbed his sleeve.

"Don't go overboard," Chip cautioned. "It's spilled milk. Let's just clean up the signs and get on with it."

"Milk!" Jamil cried. He slapped his forehead with his hand. "I totally forgot. I was on my way to buy milk for breakfast."

Chip laughed and shook his head.

"I'll pick up the signs later. I got to jet." Jamil dashed off the deck.

"Don't worry about it," Chip called after him. "I'll take care of it." He went back inside the lodge.

When Jamil went to look for Mitch at lunchtime, he had disappeared. Jamil had spent the morning working in the lodge to cool off and now he was ready to confront Mitch about the signs. As he helped set up the buffet table for the Hawaiian luau that night, he kept an eye out for Mitch or any other trouble with rude snowboarders. The afternoon, however, was uneventful.

When evening came, he planned to meet up with Nat and Kevin. A gnarly metal band, My Own Sweet, was scheduled to play outside on the deck after the luau. Around eight o'clock he stood near the buffet table, nibbling chunks of pineapple, while the band set up on the small stage. Just about everybody from school was here, including the school's principal, Mrs. Higgins.

"Aloha, dude," Nat said as she and Kevin approached Jamil. "Didn't see you on the slopes today."

Jamil shook his head. "I had chores to do around the lodge. Then I helped out with setting up the luau." Jamil poked a toothpick into a piece of pineapple. "But you won't believe what happened this morning." He explained about Chip finding the messed-up signs.

Just then, Kevin came weaving through the crowd. "I saw those signs. I thought they were funny."

"Yeah, that's what my dad would have thought, too." Jamil paused. "Not!"

"Good thing Chip replaced them," Nat said.

Kevin watched their principal doing a hula. "Guess Mrs. Higgins rocks." He laughed.

"Naw, she's here for the roast pig," Nat said. "Look, she must be wearing twenty leis."

"What a party animal," Kevin added. "Let's get closer to the stage before the crowd pushes forward."

The three of them elbowed their way through the crowd until Jamil spotted Corey Blake, the most awesome shredder on the World Cup Tour. He grabbed Nat's jacket and pointed.

"What's he doing here?" Nat asked.

"I thought he was on tour with the World Cup," Kevin added. "Isn't there an event in France this weekend?"

"Yeah, but he must be taking a break," Jamil said. "Let's go talk to him." He hurried through the crowd toward Blake with Nat and Kevin close behind him.

Blake was talking to a couple of people when Jamil interrupted them. "Would you sign my neck?" Jamil asked. He held out a marker.

"Sure, dude," Blake answered with a laugh. "This is my first neck." He took the marker and inscribed Jamil's neck with his signature. "Don't wash it off, now."

"You won't have to worry about that," Nat cracked. "He never washes his neck."

"You got that right," Jamil replied. He pulled the collar of his jacket up.

"Why aren't you on tour?" Kevin asked.

Blake looked at his friends and shrugged as if to say he was sorry for the interruption from his fans. "Just needed a rest and Chip asked me to stop by. So I'm here." He gave his goatee a little tug.

"You're friends with Chip?" Jamil exclaimed.

"Sure," Blake replied. "His family and mine have been friends forever."

Just then, My Own Sweet started warming up for the concert.

"Thanks for the autograph," Jamil said.

Jamil and his friends headed to the edge of the stage. "I can't believe Corey Blake is here," Jamil repeated. "He's going to be impossible to beat in the boardercross. I thought Mitch was going to be my toughest competition."

"Thanks," Nat replied. "What am I, burnt toast?"

Jamil faked sniffing at her. "You do have that distinct aroma."

"He's going to leave us eating snow." Kevin grinned. "I can't wait to see him ride."

My Own Sweet played a really tight set with songs from their latest album. The entire resort was rocking. Kids from all over were dancing and jamming to the awesome tunes. Jamil was so charged that he sang at the top of his voice along with My Own Sweet. By the end of the set he was completely hoarse.

"I've got to get something to drink," he rasped to his friends. He disappeared into the crowd and headed for the cooler where sodas were being sold. As he pushed through a tightly packed group, the waistband of Jamil's snow pants got snagged on something. He tried to pull away, but he was caught. He automatically reached behind to unhook himself and grabbed a hand. It was holding onto the waistband of his pants. Jamil spun around and was face to face with Mitch.

"Wedgie!" Mitch grinned.

Jamil yanked himself free. His face flushed as he saw everyone staring at him.

"Take a chill pill." Mitch raised his hands in a sign of peace.

"Back off," Jamil spat at him. He adjusted the waistband of his snow pants. "Beat it."

"Don't worry," Mitch answered. "I will, I will." He paused. "But not before I have a little fun."

"What's that supposed to mean?" Jamil asked.

"Following the boarder rules," Mitch said taunting Jamil. "You know, always cut off boring skiers, never give ski nerds the right of way. . . . Boarders rule!"

"Not like that they don't." Jamil grimaced as he got in Mitch's face. "I know about your stunt with the signs this morning, and you're not going to get away with it."

Mitch pushed Jamil away. "I don't know what you're talking about." He spread his arms out dramatically. "I'm innocent."

"Take him out, Mitch!" someone from the crowd suddenly yelled.

"Yeah, Mitch," another kid added. "Tenderize the chicken."

Mitch laughed and started toward Jamil when Wall came up beside Mitch.

"Cool it," Wall whispered.

Mitch hesitated for a minute. But someone in the

crowd threw an empty soda can at Mitch. In a flash, Mitch was on Jamil. Together they went flying across the deck and landed dead center in the huge bowl of fruit punch. The table collapsed underneath them and glasses shattered as they smashed to the ground.

5

Total chaos raged and most of the crowd pushed and shoved their way off the deck.

Jamil lay on his back with Mitch sitting on his chest.

"Back off!" Wall yelled at Mitch. "Don't be a jerk!"

Suddenly, Wall was pushed aside and Mr. Smith grabbed Mitch by the shoulders and pulled him off Jamil. "Stand over there!" he shouted as he pointed to the other side of the deck. "I'll talk to you in a minute."

Mrs. Smith slipped in front of her husband and pulled Jamil to his feet. "Are you all right?"

Jamil nodded. He couldn't believe this was happening.

"How did this start?" Mr. Smith commanded.

"I'm not sure," Jamil answered. "I was just trying to talk to Mitch and then it got out of hand." He hung his head, unable to look his dad in the eye.

"This is exactly what I've been afraid of ever since I scheduled the boarder events," Mr. Smith said. "I didn't think boarders could handle themselves." He sighed, trying to calm himself down. "And I was right."

Jamil gulped.

"But I didn't think you would be at the center of it all," Mr. Smith continued. "I'm going to have to cancel the boarder events."

"Dad!" Jamil gasped.

A murmur went through the crowd like a wave.

Mrs. Smith came up and pulled her husband aside. "Ned," she cautioned in a low voice, "you can't change the schedule this late. We have boarders from all over ready to compete."

"Yeah," Jamil added, "Corey Blake is here."

"It'll turn into a publicity disaster," Mrs. Smith said, "especially after yesterday's article in the *News*."

Mr. Smith seemed to deflate.

"What if the kids apologize and pay for the damages by working at the carnival?" Mrs. Smith suggested.

"But this is definitely the last warning." Mr. Smith relented.

"Dad, you can't believe how sorry I am," Jamil said.

"Me, too," Mitch said reluctantly as he came back across the deck.

"I'll help with the carnival, too," Wall piped in.

Jamil stared at Wall with stunned admiration. He didn't have to do that.

Then, My Own Sweet came back on stage and cranked up an awesome wall of sound.

* * *

27

Six o'clock Sunday morning, Jamil, Wall, and Mitch arrived at the maintenance office as ordered.

Chip looked up from a pile of work requisitions and started right in. "I want you to scrape the ice off the steps to the lodge, sweep the cafeteria, help reorganize the rental shop, wash the windows in the dining area, and police the grounds for trash—for starters."

"Starters?" Jamil gulped.

"Yeah, starters," Chip continued. "Mitch, why don't you check the grounds for litter, while Jamil and Wall do an equipment check at each lift." He handed Jamil a checklist. "Then I'll see what you can do next."

As Jamil and Wall reached lift number one, Jamil noticed a BOARDER RULES sign all marked up with red ink. He panicked. The signs had been vandalized again. He hurried back to the maintenance office.

"Chip," Jamil called, "someone's messed with the signs again."

Chip slapped his forehead. "That's right! I said I would take care of it. I just forgot to replace the ruined ones yesterday. I guess I got distracted."

Jamil took a deep breath to calm himself down. He wondered if his dad had seen them. "These signs could be the straw that breaks the camel's back," Jamil said. "Last night my dad said if anything else happened, he was going to cancel the boarding events."

"Yeah, I heard," Chip replied. "I've still got the extra signs right here." He picked up a small stack of signs.

"Why don't Wall and I replace them before we check

Xtreme Athletes
Rippey Shreds!

Snowboarder Jim Rippey

When Jim Rippey moved to Tahoe, California, in 1989 to work as a ski-lift operator, he had no idea that what he saw on the slopes would lead him to professional snowboarding. When he first started, he could only snowboard at night at a local resort and it was still a couple of months before he could save up enough money to buy his own board. And then one day he got a chance to see the Burton team. He watched them and realized, "What job could be better than that?"

Now, less than ten years later, Jim is one of the top five snowboarders in the world. He competed a lot as an amateur, and earned the respect of snowboarding pros. Now he can pick and choose where and when he wants to compete, but you'll be sure to see him at the Winter X Games!

Jim lives in Truckee, California.

RIPPEY'S SNOWBOARDING SAFETY TIPS

First and foremost, take a lesson!
•Wear a helmet.
•Be smart, and that means being aware and looking where you're headed.

Jim at age 6

Age: 27

Most memorable competition: The 1997 Air & Style Competition in Innsbruck, Austria. It's been going on for five years, and I was the first American to win it . . . in front of 35,000 people.

Favorite Athlete: Michael Jordan, because he is amazing.

Favorite snowboard: The Rippey Mission 156 from Burton

What I like best about my sport: I think it's the most fun sport I've ever participated in.

Favorite thing to do on a Saturday: Snowboard!

Favorite pig-out food: Ice cream

Favorite movie: *Star Wars*

the lifts," Jamil suggested. "That way if my dad hasn't seen them yet, he won't."

"Good idea," Chip confirmed.

As they began replacing signs at the lifts, Jamil turned to Wall. "So, why'd you show up this morning? You weren't fighting."

Wall shrugged and swung one of the chairs hanging from the cable. "It seemed like the right thing to do," he said hesitantly. "My dad always tells me to do what I think is right."

"Then why do you hang out with Mitch?" Jamil countered. He was ripping down a sign and taping up another.

The barb visibly stung Wall. Even though he was bigger and a year older than Jamil, the way he held himself made him seem smaller and younger. "Mitch is all right once you get to know him." Wall taped a sign up on another post. "Besides, he's an awesome boarder. He's fun to ride with."

"But he's all show," Jamil argued. "He's more interested in swag than good riding."

"Maybe," Wall replied. "But he was the only person who spoke to me on my first day of school." He headed to the next lift.

"You've only lived here a couple of weeks, right?" Jamil said as he followed Wall.

"Yeah," Wall replied. "My dad's an avalanche expert. We moved here so he can become the Rocky Mountain regional director for the National Weather Service."

"Wow!" Jamil exclaimed. "Sounds like a cool job."

"It is, but it means he travels a lot in the winter," Wall explained. "And ever since my mom took off, I've pretty much had to hang out by myself. We lived in the woods behind Barton Mountain."

"Not anymore," Jamil replied as he gave Wall a friendly slap on the back. "Come on. There are more signs in the locker room."

Jamil wanted to check the signs inside the lodge, even though he figured they hadn't been vandalized. His dad hadn't mentioned them.

"So," Jamil continued, "since you're such a good friend of Mitch, do you know anything about the signs being messed with?"

"Uh . . . ," Wall began. Then he quickly became quiet and looked away from Jamil. He shook his head. "No," he answered.

It seemed obvious that Wall was lying. But before Jamil could press Wall, he spotted something red in the snow outside the lodge. Jamil walked over and picked up a bright-red marker. The same color as the ink on the vandalized signs!

6

Jamil studied the marker more closely. There was nothing strange about it, except for the fact that it had some kind of logo on it, mountain peaks interspersed with snowflakes.

"Look at this!" Jamil exclaimed, holding up the marker for Wall to see.

Wall didn't even come over to look at it. "I see," he said. "Anyone could have dropped that," Wall added with his eyes riveted on the snow at his feet. "Thousands of people came through here yesterday."

"But Mitch is supposed to have cleaned their mess up," Jamil countered. "Look." He waved his hand. "The place is spotless, except for this marker."

Wall followed his hand.

"Someone must have dropped it in the last few minutes," Jamil argued. He looked at his watch. "And it's still an hour before the slopes open."

"Maybe." Wall grunted. He just kept his eyes glued to a mound of snow at his feet.

Jamil gave Wall a sidelong glance. What's he so uptight about? he thought. He's not being accused of anything. But Wall was definitely acting suspicious. Maybe he does have something to hide.

"Come on," Jamil said marching back to the lifts. "We've got to run through this checklist."

Around lunchtime, Jamil spotted Nat and Kevin carrying their snowboards toward the chairlift.

"Hey!" Jamil called. He waved as he leaned his push broom against the railing on the deck.

Nat and Kevin detoured toward Jamil.

"Hey, dude," Kevin greeted Jamil.

"S'up?" Nat said with a grin. "How's the work? Do you feel fully reformed from your evil ways?"

"Something like that," Jamil answered. "Hey, you guys riding?"

"Yup," Kevin said as he leaned on his board. "Us law-abiding citizens are going to enjoy our freedom on the slopes."

"Give me five minutes," Jamil said. He quickly swept the deck clean and ran inside to get his boots and board.

"You been paroled?" Kevin cracked.

"Hey, look!" Nat shouted excitedly. "TV cameras!"

"Looks like they're taping Blake coming down the mountain," Kevin observed.

Nat started toward the cameras. "Come on."

A crowd was already forming around Blake and the camera crew.

"This is a circus," Kevin said.

"My dad'll like this!" Jamil replied as he caught up with them. "Wait here while I get my boots on." Jamil sat in the snow and untied his sneakers.

"How was the work?" Nat asked.

"Oh, you know," Jamil replied. "But one thing turned up." He reached into his pocket and pulled out the red marker. "I found this around where Mitch was working this morning."

"A clue," Kevin said. "You think Mitch did the signs?"

"Could be," Jamil said. "But Wall was acting really weird this morning, too. Either he's got something to hide or he's in with Mitch."

"Okay Mr. Detective," Kevin replied. "But remember what happened the last time you solved a mystery."

"Yeah," Nat said, laughing. "He thought that there was a ring of snowboard thieves among the kitchen staff."

Jamil blushed. "Well how was I supposed to know they were doing board maintenance on the side?"

"All I'm saying is, let's not jump to conclusions just yet," Kevin replied.

"Yes, O Logical One," Jamil said with an exaggerated bow.

"But really, Jamil might have something here," Nat said. "It could be Mitch. Wall might be involved, but Mitch is the only certified jerk who would pull a stunt like that." Nat took the marker and held it up.

"Wall is giving me really strange vibes, too," Jamil persisted.

"But now we have evidence," said Nat.

"Not yet," Kevin cautioned. "First, we've got to connect the marker to Mitch or Wall."

"You're right," Nat said, "Mitch or Wall might mess with the signs, but it doesn't mean that either would have faxed the paper. They spend all their time at Hoke Valley. It's got the best trails. They wouldn't want to put a wrench in it for riders."

"You're forgetting how the article seemed like it was quoting Mitch," Jamil said. "But I guess you're right. Not everything adds up. And I'm certain Wall knows something."

Jamil put the marker back in his pocket and zipped his jacket. "There's more to it than Mitch messing up signs. I just need to find out what it is before Hoke Valley is ruined for boarders."

"Or, with more bad publicity, ruined for skiers, too," Kevin added.

"Let's ride," Nat suggested.

Good idea, Jamil thought. He needed something to take his mind off these problems.

But before they could go for their boards, they heard a loud rumbling sound coming from the rental shop below the lodge's deck.

"*Heeeelllppp!*" A high-pitched scream pierced the air.

The crew rushed over, but they couldn't get in the shop. Something was blocking the door.

"Give me a hand," Kevin said as he put his shoulder against the door. He turned the door handle and the three of them shoved the door open a crack. "One, two, three, push!" The door swung open wide enough for them to slip in. A pile of skis was blocking the door. They scrambled over the them and gasped.

Standing in the middle of chaos was Julie Newburg, the rental clerk. She had her hands up to her mouth, and she seemed to be in shock. "Oh, no! Oh, no!" she whispered over and over again.

The shop was demolished. Skis and equipment had been thrown everywhere. Broken skis and bindings were piled thickly against the door to the outside. But strangely enough, none of the boarding equipment was touched.

Jamil led Julie over to a stool behind the counter. "What happened?"

Julie gulped. "Every day at this time I leave the shop for ten minutes. Just to grab a sandwich." Julie paused as she surveyed the mess. "And today, when I got back, I unlocked the door and someone was inside trashing the place."

"Did you get a good look at who it was?" Jamil asked.

"Yes. I mean, no," Julie answered. She ran her hand through her long brown hair. "I saw him. At least I think it was a him, but he was wearing a dark ski mask and dark ski clothes, so I can't be sure who it was."

"Anything else?" Kevin broke in.

Julie shook her head. "Just that he had destroyed the place, especially the ski equipment." She looked up and pointed at the mess. Her small shoulders slumped beneath her green reindeer sweater.

"Did you see where he went?" Jamil pressed.

"No. He disappeared into the crowd around the lockers outside the rental shop," Julie said. "The place was packed with skiers." She shook her head in disbelief. "I better call security." Julie picked up her phone and dialed.

Jamil turned from her and saw someone lurking by the door that they just came through.

The person started to enter. "Hi!" She held up her press card. "I'm Debbie Windsor, with the *News*."

Jamil ignored her greeting and slammed the door in her face. He looked over at Nat. "The last thing my dad needs is more bad publicity."

Kevin leaned against the counter and asked Julie,

"Was the door locked?"

Julie nodded. "And it was still locked when I came back."

"Then how did the person get inside?" Jamil asked as he looked over his shoulder to make sure the reporter didn't return.

"I'm not sure. He must have had a key," Julie replied.

"Could he have hid inside, then waited for you to leave?" Nat asked.

"Maybe," Julie said, "but I think I'd know if someone was in here with me."

"Hmmm," Nat replied as she scratched her chin thoughtfully. "It must be an inside job."

"You've got to be kidding!" Jamil choked out.

"The person knew her routine," Nat argued.

Jamil shook his head. "Who was in the shop before you closed it?" he asked Julie.

Julie paused to think. "That snowboarder with the goatee," Julie said. "I can't remember his name, but he bragged to me that he won a World Cup."

"Corey Blake?" Kevin gasped.

"That's him!" Julie said. "He was checking out the latest snap-in bindings. Also, Mitch was here helping me clean up."

"Really? Mitch?" Jamil said. "That's it! This time the jerk has gone too far."

"Wait a minute," Nat said. "Julie, what else do you remember?"

"Well, Chip assigned him to help me in here this

morning," Julie said. "And just before lunch a friend of Mitch's showed up."

"Who?" Jamil asked expectantly.

Julie shook her head. "I don't know him. He's new or something."

"What'd he look like?" Kevin prodded.

"He was taller than Mitch." Julie paused. "And he wore a green ski jacket and black snow pants."

"Wall!" Jamil exclaimed. "But what was he doing here? He told me he was heading home for lunch."

"Julie, you said it was one person, not two," Kevin countered.

Julie nodded.

"So it's either Mitch or Wall, not both," continued Kevin.

"Or one of the rogue boarders mentioned in the paper, or Corey Blake, or someone who works here," Nat added.

Just then, Mr. Smith entered the shop with the resort's security guard "Oh, no!" Mr. Smith groaned. "What happened now?"

Julie explained, while Jamil, Nat, and Kevin tried to stay out of Mr. Smith's way. They could tell he was ready to blow, and they didn't want it directed toward them.

The shop was a total disaster. It was going to take more than a couple of hours to clean the mess up. As Jamil picked up skis, he could tell that they were going to have to be retuned. There were huge gouges in them, and the edges were nicked and dulled.

After Julie finished, Mr. Smith surveyed the mess. "We're going to have to close the rental shop until tomorrow. I don't want anyone in here while we clean up."

"We'll help," Nat volunteered.

Jamil gave her a dirty look. Nat was always volunteering herself—and Jamil and Kevin, sometimes without their consent. Sure, it was nice to help out, but he'd rather board.

"I can't believe this is happening in the middle of carnival week," Mr. Smith said. "I've got a million things to do. I appreciate your help, kids. Julie will tell you what needs to be done." Mr. Smith headed back to his office with the guard.

Jamil, Kevin, and Nat dug through the mess, putting things back where they belonged. They stacked the skis that needed repair along one wall.

After a few minutes, Chip stuck his head in the shop. "What happened?" His hair was tousled, as if he'd been sleeping.

Jamil explained.

"This is a disaster!" Chip replied.

Kevin tried to play it down. "Not if we get it cleaned up fast."

Julie handed Jamil a file and asked him to begin sharpening the ski edges. She went over and pulled out an iron and some strips of plastic to patch the gouges in the skis. "Don't worry," Julie said, trying to smile. "It's not as bad as it looks. We can fix everything."

Jamil looked relieved and set to work on the skis. "It's

got to be Mitch. This is just the kind of stunt he'd pull."

"Just like the signs," Nat added. She was putting back together a sunglasses display.

"I don't know," Kevin said. "This is way too hardcore for Mitch. There's more to it than just the signs and the rental shop. What about the article in the *News*? And how did that reporter know to be here when the shop was destroyed?"

"Mitch is a jerk," Jamil asserted. "I think he'd do anything to cause problems."

"But how did the reporter know to come here this morning?" Kevin repeated. "No, somebody is contacting her, and that seems more than Mitch would be interested in. He'd go for the yucks."

"This seems like a prank to me," Nat said, stopping her work to glance across the shop at Jamil.

Chip stopped filing as he listened to their conversation. "It's just kids goofing," Chip added.

"This seems like more than just goofing. There's a lot of damage here." Kevin dug his feet in. "Besides, there are other suspects. Corey Blake was in here, too. And what is he doing here anyway? He should be on the World Cup tour. And what about Wall? He's new. And none of this happened until he showed up."

"Corey's a friend. I asked him to come to help promote the boarding events," Chip replied. "He's hardcore, but he's all right."

Now Jamil was really confused. He needed to think this thing out. He silently filed the edge of a ski for a few minutes. "And then there's that reporter. She's got to be involved."

Nat nodded. "And what about all the skiers who would love to see boarding banned."

"Yeah, you're right," Kevin admitted. "But that just means that we're searching for a needle in a haystack. It's going to be impossible."

"I've got to fire up the grill for the barbeque tonight," Chip said as he left.

Jamil leaned over the ski he was working on and the red marker fell out of his pocket. Before it hit the ground, a lightbulb went off in his head. "The marker! I know where that logo is from!"

"It's from Barton Mountain!" Jamil said as he reached over and picked up the marker.

Nat looked at him as if he was speaking Latin.

"You know," Jamil continued, "that funky little ski slope about fifty miles down the road."

"I know which ski slope you mean," Nat said impatiently. "But what has Barton Mountain got to do with anything?"

"I don't know," Jamil replied, "but it's a start. It's a clear lead. We should check it out."

"You mean go over to Barton?" Kevin asked, not quite believing what he was hearing. "It's fifty miles from here! How are we going to get there?"

"I don't know," Jamil answered. "But it's as solid a lead as we have."

"Wait a second," Nat said as she slapped her forehead. "Wall is from Barton!"

Kevin snorted in disbelief. "You're getting too carried

away with this detective stuff. Anybody could have dropped that marker. Any number of the thousands of people who come here could have gone to Barton Mountain first, and then dropped the marker in the snow. It wasn't necessarily left by the person who vandalized the signs."

"But the vandals wrote in red," Jamil argued.

Nat glared at Kevin. "Do you have any better ideas? Or are you just going to poke holes in ours?"

Kevin shook his head. "Okay, I'll admit it's a lead, but I'm not ready to say it's Wall. I mean, what's his motive?"

"Well, we don't know for sure, but we *do* know the marker came from Barton, so it's worth going up there to check it out," Nat concluded. "Now, all we have to do is find a ride."

"Meet me in front of the lodge at eight tomorrow morning," Jamil told them. "I have an idea."

Later that afternoon, as Jamil left the shop, he spotted the reporter Debbie Windsor chatting up a skier. Though Jamil couldn't hear what she was saying, he could tell she was peppering the skier with questions.

"Why don't you back off," Jamil called to her. "There's no story here."

Debbie turned and smiled when she saw Jamil. "Just the person I wanted to talk to. You're Ned Smith's son, right?"

Jamil nodded warily and took a step backward.

"What's the real story behind Hoke Valley?" she asked. "How do snowboarders feel about the rogue boarders?"

"Nothing," Jamil said defensively. "What are you trying to make up?"

"Make up?" Debbie replied, a little surprised. "Sources of mine tipped me to today's disaster at the rental shop. And a fax I received several days ago put me on to the whole snowboarder mess. I'd say there's a story here."

Jamil held up his hands and backed away. "You already have your mind made up."

After his conversation with Debbie, Jamil decided to do what he always did when he was upset. Board. It always made the worst situations seem not so bad. Once someone asked him what he thought about when he was riding, and he couldn't say. He didn't remember ever thinking of anything while he shredded. So now was the perfect time to strap in and carve. He grabbed his board and rode the lift to the top of Mount Olley.

The clouds were inching in close, about to encircle the peak. Their presence hung over Jamil like the weight of the events of the last two days. He stomped his right boot onto his board to knock off snow and strapped in. As he sat in the snow at the top of the slope, his eyes rested on a sticker on the nose of his board: QUESTION REALITY! SNOWBOARD, DUDE!

He grunted at the thought of questioning reality. It seemed as if his dad had been questioning his reality about snowboarding ever since he started boarding. He flopped over on his hands and knees and pushed himself onto his board. He twisted to turn his board downslope and rode.

His body quickly took over and hurled down the fall

line, while his mind emptied of his troubles. The only things he was aware of were his muscles contracting and releasing with each move and adjustment. He was in perfect sync, barely aware of his movements.

He stuck a solid indy three and rode into a Bertle, his body parallel to the slope. Then, he popped up and hucked a bonk for some big air. He grabbed a perfect swany method and boned it out.

He jostled a little, then stomped the landing.

"All right!" someone on the slopes cried.

Jamil raised his hand in acknowledgment and continued on. He compressed to a tight crouch and punched a gnarlie ollie in the flat bowl of the slope. He sailed down the rest of the slope in a zone where no rogue boarder could enter.

Early Monday morning, Jamil, Kevin, and Nat gathered by the entrance to the lodge's kitchen.

"We'll just wait for the Mighty Buns truck," Jamil explained. "Bob Wittingham drives it. His route goes right past Barton, and he returns to Hoke Valley. My dad gives him a free pass every year, so he shouldn't mind doing us a favor."

Just then, the Mighty Buns truck pulled up to the lodge. In a matter of minutes, Jamil, Kevin, and Nat were sitting on the floor in the back of the truck riding to Barton Mountain.

After a few stops at restaurants along the way, Bob pulled into the Barton Mountain parking lot to deliver a load of bread. He promised to pick them up around noon and drive them back to Hoke Valley.

As the gang stood in front of the Barton Mountain lodge, Nat shivered. "This place gives me the creeps," Nat said. "Look, the parking lot isn't even half full."

"And the lodge looks like it's about to collapse," Kevin added. "They should close this place down."

"Hey!" Jamil said, pointing to some construction by the slopes. "It looks like they're building a new lift."

The crew entered the lodge and were surprised to see that the inside was brand-new. The entire lodge had been redone—new floors, new wall paneling, new lighting.

"This place looks great!" Nat said.

"I wonder where they got the money to do this," Kevin said. "Not from visitors, that's for sure."

"I don't think we have to worry about Barton Mountain skiers," Jamil cracked. "Coming here has got to be the all-time dumbest idea ever."

Nat glowered at Jamil. "Zip it!"

"What are we going to learn here?" Kevin asked. "The problem is at Hoke Valley."

"We're here," Nat replied. "Let's make the best of it. Where's the office?"

Kevin pointed to a sign with an arrow directing them up the stairs. The office door was open.

An old man sat behind a desk sipping coffee.

"What can I do for you?" he asked them.

Jamil and Nat looked at each other. They realized they didn't really have a plan.

"We were wondering about buying used equipment," Jamil blurted out. It was the first thing he thought of.

"Well, let me see," the old man replied. "We don't have anything for sale right now, but at the end of the season we'll be getting rid of all our rentals. My son, Melvin, is planning to take the place over in the fall and completely renovate it."

"We saw that some of the work has already started," Jamil said to encourage the old man to talk.

"Yes, it has," the old man said as he stood to look out the window. "Barton Mountain was owned by my wife's family. She and I ran it for fifty years. After she died eleven years ago, I tried to keep it going until Melvin could take it over, but I'm not gifted at it like my wife, Marlene, was." He seemed to drift off into memories of the past.

"So your son is going to run it?" Jamil prodded.

"That's right," the old man answered. "He's got a slew of plans." A look of pride crossed his face. "He thinks he can turn Barton into some kind of hot place for kids. He keeps talking about snowboarding, but I think it's just a fad. You need to stick with what's worked. And that's skiing."

Jamil and his friends let the old man ramble on. Jamil could see how his son had the right idea. The only way Barton Mountain was going to survive was if they got new visitors. As he listened, Jamil envied the pride the old man expressed in his son. His own dad didn't seem to respect anything he did.

Kevin nudged Jamil and directed his gaze toward a red marker lying on the old man's desk. It had the same mountain and snowflake logo on it as the one Jamil had found.

Nat noticed the logo, too. She pulled on her friends' sleeves and motioned to leave.

"Uh," Jamil said politely. "I think we've got to go. But first, I was wondering if you knew the Evans family. They used live near here."

The old man tapped his fingers on his desk as he thought. Then he shook his head. "Not that I can recall."

"Thanks. We'll check in at the end of the season about the equipment," Jamil said as he and his friends left.

The old man smiled and waved. He sat back down at his desk and proceeded to sign some papers.

Outside, the crew sat on a bench by the parking lot waiting for Bob and the Mighty Buns truck.

"I guess it was just a fishing expedition," Nat admitted to her friends.

"Yeah," Kevin replied. "Nothing much, except for confirming the logo on the marker."

"And it still doesn't mean anything," Nat said, obviously disappointed.

"I tell you it's Mitch," Jamil said firmly.

"Or Wall," Nat added.

Jamil nodded. They had to admit that no other suspect really seemed to make sense.

"Arrrrriiiibbba!" the DJ shouted above the pulsing sounds of Caribbean salsa music.

Jamil's dad had hung a mirrored disco ball above the lodge's deck, and positioned large heaters along the edges. As skiers came down off the slopes, they were greeted by resort personnel, dressed in shorts and T-shirts over their long underwear, handing out brightly colored fruit drinks.

Jamil surveyed this from behind the grill where he was helping Chip cook chicken and giant shrimp. The night skiing tickets included the Caribbean Night dinner and events.

Then Jamil spotted his mom and dad dancing up a storm in the middle of the crowded deck. He covered his face with his hands and peaked through his fingers. "This is embarrassing." He groaned. "They are so corny."

Chip laughed.

"I don't think I can take a night of this awful music,"

Jamil complained to Chip, "or my parents making fools of themselves." Jamil hung his tongs on the grill handle. He frowned as he spotted Mitch and Wall stading by the deck's steps holding large fruity drinks with umbrellas poking out.

"Why don't you hit the slopes, then," Chip replied. "You didn't get any riding in today. And tomorrow is the big air."

Jamil took off his apron and hung it on the deck's railing behind him. "You're right. I could definitely do a little shredding."

"I've got it under control," Chip said as he flipped a couple of chickens.

Jamil started around the grill when he tripped and nearly fell into the fire. As he caught himself, he groaned. "On second thought, I think I'd better go home. I've been up since dawn two mornings in a row. I'm beat."

"Whatever," Chip said. "See you tomorrow."

"Thanks," Jamil said. He knew that once his head hit the pillow he was going to be out like a light.

In his room, Jamil loaded his favorite My Own Sweet CD and cranked the sound to drown out the music from the carnival. This is much better than salsa music, he thought. He laid on his bed and leafed through the latest issue of *Shredder*. To his surprise, he turned immediately to a photo of Corey Blake coming off a humongous cliff with a toe grab.

He wondered again why Corey would be here in Hoke Valley. He scanned the interview on the opposite page.

SHREDDER: So what's next?

BLAKE: My own snowboard park. I'm investing in a friend's ski resort, and we're turning it into a boarder's-only resort.

SHREDDER: About time someone did that. Where?

BLAKE: Barton Mountain, Colorado.

"Whaaa?" Jamil screamed. His eyes nearly popped out of his head.

Ring! Ring! The telephone interrupted.

Jamil jumped up and ran downstairs to grab the phone in the kitchen. "Yeah?" he said into the receiver.

"Uh," the voice said. It took on a menacing edge. "Stop poking around, or someone's going to get hurt."

"Who is this?" Jamil demanded.

"Remember," the voice said angrily, "if you don't back off, someone's going to fall down and not get up on Freight Train run."

SLAM! Jamil hung up the phone with a bang. Freight Train was Hoke Valley's notorious double black-diamond trail and the site of both the boardercross and the big air competitions. The last thing he wanted to happen was another disaster. That would seal the coffin on boarding at Hoke Valley forever.

He immediately picked up the phone and dialed star-six-nine. His hands shook. That phone call rattled him to the core. After a few rings a recording told him that the number could not be reached with call return—the mysterious caller must have used a pay phone. He hung up and dialed Nat, but her family's answering machine picked up. Jamil then dialed Kevin's number. He wasn't home either. They were probably still at Caribbean Night.

Jamil looked out the window and saw the flashing lights through the trees and heard the thumping bass echoing through the valley. He debated whether to go over and try to find them, then decided it wasn't worth it.

Instead, he ran upstairs and booted up his computer. He could E-mail them. He had to tell them about both Corey Blake and the phone call. Nat and Kevin always checked their E-mail before they went to bed.

After he sent them both long messages, he was too keyed up to go to bed, so he stayed on line and played Zorched! He also set up a buddy watch so he'd know if either Nat or Kevin checked their E-mail when they got home.

While he waited for his friends, Jamil selected the character of the evil Monk of Bathsheba. He stole an incantation from Merlin, but unfortunately he used it incorrectly. Every step he took forward, the world behind him disintegrated. At the same time, reality kept reconfiguring as if someone were spinning a wheel of fortune. One moment he would be in a forest. His next step, however, would land him in a traffic-clogged city. Jamil couldn't figure out how to break the spell, so he slowly moved forward, unable to find a map to pinpoint where he was in the game. When the flesh-eating gnomes appeared, he knew that with no way to retreat, he was about to be Zorched!

Luckily, it wasn't long before a happy face icon started blinking in the upper right hand corner of his screen. Underneath the smiling face the name NAT appeared.

Nat had logged on.

Jamil exited Zorched! and keyed in an "immediate message," telling her to meet him in a chat room.

NAT: Whoa! Who do you think was on the phone?

JAMIL: No clue.

NAT: Just ignore it. It's got to be Mitch trying to shake you up before the big air tomorrow night.

JAMIL: Maybe. But this person seemed serious. I don't think he was kidding around.

The chat room suddenly indicated that Kevin had joined them.

JAMIL: Hey, Kev. So what do you think?

KEVIN: I don't like it, but it's not something we can worry about.

JAMIL: Things seem to be getting out of control.

NAT: It's just a practical joke.

JAMIL: But what do you make of Corey Blake

being here?

KEVIN: What do you mean?

JAMIL: I mean, Corey is here at Hoke Valley, but he's now Hoke Valley's competition. What's he doing here?

KEVIN: If you're so worried, why don't you tell your dad about it.

JAMIL: Yeah, and get the boarding events canceled. Fat chance. We have to deal with it ourselves.

Around midnight, Jamil tossed and turned in his bed. He couldn't fall asleep. He was still shaken by the phone call, and he didn't have a clue about what to do. He could still hear the Caribbean music drifting across the woods to his upstairs bedroom, but the steady beat didn't soothe Jamil. He couldn't seem to shake the feeling that the caller meant what he said. That something terrible was really going to happen.

Tuesday morning was a bright sunny day. The light reflected off the snow, creating an almost blinding glare. Everyone at the resort was wearing their darkest sunglasses.

Jamil stood on his condominium's front stoop, spreading sand. On these early spring days, the sun melted the snow just enough so that every night a sheet of ice formed on the surface of nearly everything.

This morning he felt a little better. A night's sleep, even a bad one, could have a calming effect. In the light of day he wanted to convince himself that it was Mitch or Wall who was behind the stuff going on at Hoke Valley. It just seemed too crazy that it could be Blake. Then it would mean Blake was trying to ruin boarding at Hoke Valley.

When he was done spreading sand, Jamil headed over to the Mount Olley chairlift with his snowboard. He was supposed to meet Chip up at the top to lay out

Wednesday's boardercross course and set up the crowd barriers for that night's big air. Mitch and Wall were supposed to help, too. Jamil was anxious to see how they reacted when he saw him this morning. He wanted to see if he could somehow trip them up. Were they worrying together? Jamil wasn't sure.

As Jamil slid down the lift ramp, he was thrilled at the conditions. "Shagadelic!" he said. The snow was perfect corn snow, a granular condition that only occurs in the early spring. It made for a fabulous ride.

Jamil looked around for Chip and the others, but didn't see them. He was early, so he decided to take advantage of the conditions and get a little shredding in. He quickly strapped on his board, hopped so he was pointing downhill, and took off.

Jamil went straight down the fall line to pick up speed. Then he took a steep Eurocarve, dragging his hand along the snow. Powder sprayed in an elegant wide arc. In one fluid motion he turned cross slope and hucked a massive bonk. He lifted his knees, bringing his board up to his chest. His right hand dropped. He reached for his tail, grabbed, and gave it a quick tweak. His purple board flashed in the sunlight. He landed in time to cut to the left around a tight bend to Freight Train's steepest part.

As he whipped around, he discovered he had no place to go. A massive caterpillar, a snow-packing machine with threads like a tank, was tearing up the slope directly in front of him! It was about to turn him into hardpack!

Jamil sat and slid straight down toward the grinding

caterpillar treads. He was totally out of control.

"Aggghhh!" Jamil screamed. He gulped for air like he was drowning. All he could see were the treads of the cat grinding up the snow like chopped meat. In one second he'd be hamburger.

But then the cat veered to the right and Jamil rolled to safety.

Jamil collapsed on the slope and unbuckled his boots. His whole body was shaking badly.

The engine of the cat shut down.

Jamil took a couple of deep breaths. "Hey!" he yelled. "You almost turned me into roadkill!"

The door to the cat opened and the driver climbed out. When he turned, Jamil almost had a heart attack. It was Mitch!

Mitch fell from the cat, laughing at the terrified expression on Jamil's face.

"You idiot!" Jamil shouted as he jumped to his feet. "You idiot!" He ran over to Mitch and stood menacingly over him. "Not only did you almost kill me, but you also could have gotten boarding banned from Hoke Valley. If my dad finds out about a boarder stealing a cat, riding is over here."

Mitch ignored him and laughed harder. "Lighten up, dude. I wasn't going to run you over. It was just a joke."

"I can live without these kinds of jokes," Jamil said as he stomped back to his board. He turned and pointed at Mitch. "You're dangerous!" Jamil pulled the red marker out of his pocket. "Not only do you vandalize signs and

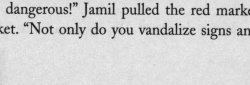

trash the rental shop, but you steal resort equipment."

"Wait a sec," Mitch said holding up his hands.

"This is your marker," Jamil continued.

"No, it isn't," Mitch said.

"It's what you used to mess with the signs," Jamil said as he breathed heavily.

"You got the wrong guy," Mitch protested. "That's Chip's marker."

Jamil was fed up. "I'm going straight to my dad about this. Now you've gone too far. If you had stopped at the signs, I might have gone easy on you. But you had to wreck the rental shop, you had to fax that dumb article to the *News*, and you had to call and threaten me last night—and now this!" Jamil shook his head in disgust. He was beyond angry. If Mitch could pull a stunt like this, then he definitely could have done the other stuff, too.

Mitch stood there stunned. "I didn't do that," he insisted. "And that's not my marker."

"I found it by a marked-up sign," Jamil replied.

As Mitch sputtered, trying to respond, Chip came around the corner.

"Hey, what's going on?" Chip said. "I could hear you from the top of the slope." He eyed the marker. "That's mine. I've been trying to get it back from Mitch." Chip took it from Jamil's hand. "But Mitch said he lost it."

Mitch slumped to the snow. "Busted," he muttered.

Jamil glared at him like he was going to eat him for dinner.

Mitch shrugged. "Yeah," he admitted. "The sign was

me. I did it."

"It?" Jamil replied. "You mean them. Almost every sign was messed with."

"Not by me," Mitch swore. "I did just one, and I didn't do the other things. Just ask Wall." He pointed up slope.

At that moment Wall was coming down the slope on his snowboard.

"What kind of nut case are you friends with?" Jamil shouted.

Wall pulled up and slid to a stop next to the group. "Huh?"

"Mitch says you'll back him up that he didn't wreck the rental shop or tip off the *Hoke Valley News* about rogue boarders," said Jamil.

Wall just looked away. He didn't answer.

"He also says you'll back him up on his messing with just *one* Boarder Rules sign," continued Jamil.

Wall grunted unintelligibly.

Jamil, Mitch, and Chip stared at him for a moment.

"Tell them," Mitch prodded.

Wall gave a half nod and shrugged.

"I swear it wasn't me!" Mitch protested.

"Let's get on with our work," Chip said to break the standoff.

But before they could leave, the *News* reporter Debbie Windsor came tromping up the slope in her snow boots. She had her tape recorder in her hand, and she looked as if she was not going to give up until she had a story.

"Not her again," Jamil moaned.

"Is it really true that Hoke Valley is no longer a safe venue to pursue winter sports?" she spoke into her tape recorder.

"Whaaa?" Jamil replied.

"Is Hoke Valley too dangerous? Are there rogue boarders threatening the safety of all who visit?" she persisted.

"You've got the wrong place, lady," Jamil answered. He bent over to pick up his board. "Sorry we can't stay and talk, but we've got work to do."

Jamil, Chip, Mitch, and Wall started climbing into the cat. They were going to ride it back up the hill.

"What about the sabotage to the rental shop yesterday?" she shouted after them. "I know that really happened. I saw it with my own eyes."

Chip turned and confirmed that someone did mess up the rental shop yesterday, but nothing was stolen and everything was repaired.

"Was someone trying to cover up the fact that Hoke Valley is renting faulty equipment?" Debbie continued, ignoring every brush-off.

"That's ridiculous!" Jamil replied.

"That's not what I hear," Debbie said. "And you can read about it in tomorrow's *News*."

Jamil stood there stunned as he watched her walk back down the mountain.

11

That night was South of the Border Night. Mr. Smith had organized a giant fiesta with a Mexican mariachi band. Piñatas of all sorts hung from wires above the deck. Colorful streamers decked the railings, windows, and doors. A buffet of soft and hard tacos, enchiladas, burritos, and other traditional dishes was piled high for everyone.

Jamil liked tacos and could stand the Mexican music, so he made plans to meet Nat and Kevin for dinner.

"What's up with your dad?" Nat asked as she approached Jamil by a large bowl of punch. "Has he gone nuts?"

"He thinks he's a genius," Jamil cracked. "I feel like I'm on some cruise ship, though."

"Let's stuff our faces," Nat said with a smile.

Jamil rubbed his stomach. "I'm starving. But first I got to tell you about what happened today."

As the two of them headed for the buffet, Jamil filled Nat in on the details of Mitch and his catepillar stunt.

While he spoke, Kevin joined them.

"Whoa!" Kevin exclaimed.

"But wait, there's more," Jamil continued. "I spoke to my dad and Mitch is now banned from Hoke Valley."

"That's rough," Nat commented.

"Yeah," Jamil agreed, "But he deserves it after all he's done."

"We'd better eat now," Kevin said as he surveyed the food. "This stuff is going to take a while to digest."

"Just make sure you eat the beans," Jamil said. "They'll give you lift on the big air."

"And stink out the competition," Nat added.

"*Olé!*" Kevin replied.

They found a table inside. No matter how hard the heaters worked, it was still freezing on the deck.

Jamil's plate was crammed tightly with six tacos. Nat chose one enchilada and some rice and refried beans. Kevin stuck with vegetables. His plate was mostly salad and salsa.

"Rabbit food," Jamil cracked as he looked at Kevin's plate.

"I'm not letting this meal weigh me down," Kevin said as he dug in. "I'm just hoping Corey Blake eats here tonight. This meal will definitely slow him down."

They laughed.

"Speaking of Blake . . ." Jamil nodded in the direction of the stairs.

Corey Blake was holding court, standing on the stairs above a crowd of people. Jamil spotted the *News* reporter

Debbie Windsor among them. Blake's voice was loud and carried across the room.

"Come over to Barton Mountain next week," Blake said, "and I'll show you a real snowboarding park." He hitched up his jeans like some gunslinger out of a western.

"Barton Mountain?" Kevin cracked. "He must be joking."

"But while I'm here," Blake continued, "I'm sure not going to let some snot-nosed amateur show me up."

"Give me a break," Nat said as she shoved a forkful of food in her mouth.

"I'm here to win," he concluded. "And nobody can catch air like me. So the rest of you might as well go home."

"What a moron," Nat said without even lifting her face from her plate. "I sure don't know why Chip is friends with him."

"I think I'll wash my neck now," Jamil cracked. "He's way too full of himself." Nat and Kevin laughed.

Jamil took a bite from a taco and glanced around the room. He didn't know many of the people here. The crowd was mostly vacationers. The locals didn't usually come out for these things. Jamil did spot Wall, however. He was sitting at the next table with some of the kids who hung around Mitch. The sight of him rang a bell and he turned to his friends. "What's with Barton Mountain?"

"Yeah, I know," Kevin replied. "Blake mentioned it, and Chip has a marker from there."

"Do they really ride that dump?" Nat asked.

"Chip probably picked it up at some regional ski meeting or from Blake," Jamil explained, "since he's a Barton owner."

"Yeah, I can't imagine anyone hanging at Barton Mountain with Hoke Valley just down the road," Kevin said. He wiped his paper plate clean with a tortilla.

"They are trying to turn it around," Nat said. "We saw them renovating the entire place, putting in a new chairlift, and a bunch of other stuff. It might be kind of cool."

"Oh, yeah," a voice interjected. They all turned around to see Wall now sitting alone at a table nearby. "That's right. I did hear something about them putting in a snowboarding park."

Jamil just stared at him.

"Rockin'!" Nat said, after a pause. "I'd sure go in a flash. I'm dying to ride the halfpipe."

"Me, too," Kevin seconded.

"It'll be great," Wall agreed as he stood up. "Well, gotta run. Catch you later."

The minute Wall was out of earshot, Jamil leaned toward his friends urgently. "Isn't it a bit odd that he knew about Barton Mountain? And that he was eavesdropping on our conversation? Could we have been wrong about Mitch? Maybe it's Wall."

His question trailed off into uneasy silence.

"ATTENTION! ATTENTION!" a voice over the loud-speaker announced. "THE BIG AIR WILL BEGIN IN EXACTLY FIFTEEN MINUTES. ALL CONTESTANTS MUST BE CHECKED IN AT THE STARTING GATE BY THEN!"

Jamil, Nat, and Kevin jumped up from the table and dashed out the door with a dozen other boarders. Jamil didn't have time to figure out what Wall was up to. He had to get his mind focused on the big air.

Flying off a jump and sailing twenty or thirty feet in the air before landing on the slope required every ounce of concentration, as well as every bit of courage.

Jamil glanced up at the full moon and hoped it was a good omen as he and his friends rode the chairlift up to the top of Mount Olley. They could see the crowd gathering on the sides of the slope and around the jump. They had to board halfway down the slope to get to the starting gate of the big air competition. Big air was essentially a jump where the boarder tried to perform as outrageous a trick as possible and land without falling. It wasn't easy, and it took nerves of steel to fly that high in the air and not panic.

Jamil closed his eyes and tried to visualize his jump, but he couldn't. Instead, the phone call from the night before, warning that trouble was in store for someone on Freight Train, dominated his thoughts. He couldn't help feeling that danger was all around him. He scanned the slope as he rode up in the chairlift. But he didn't see anything suspicious.

When they reached the top, the crew came off the lift and strapped in their back feet. They took the top half of Freight Train slowly, just trying to stretch their muscles and relax. At the gate they checked in with the starter.

When Nat learned she was first, she was relieved. "Now I can just get the jump over with and watch."

"But you won't know what you need to do without seeing the others go first," Kevin said. He was sitting on a mound of snow with his board on his lap, tightening his bindings.

"I can dig that," Jamil said. "Better to just go all out. Set the standard and let everybody else catch up."

"I can't stand waiting around," Nat replied. "I'd go nuts chewing off all my fingernails waiting for my turn. And every jump would look like something better than I could ever do."

"You're right," Kevin said with a laugh. "You'd better go first or you'll be driving us all crazy."

Jamil was no longer listening. His attention was drawn to the bottom of the jump, where someone in a dark ski parka and a mask was positioning two five gallon buckets right on the edge of the landing area. It looked like the buckets were being used to prop up the fence, but that didn't make sense. His dad never used buckets.

Jamil's attention was distracted from this when his dad walked up to the edge of the jump with a microphone in his hand. "Welcome to Hoke Valley's first ever big air! Tonight we have twenty competitors, including Corey Blake, ranked number one in boardercross on the World Cup Tour."

Blake stood by the gate and waved.

The audience applauded. Loud cheers echoed across the mountain.

"I'd better get ready," Nat said as she slid over to the gate. She strapped in her back foot and positioned herself down the fall line.

"Let's rock and roll!" Mr. Smith shouted into the mike.

Loud music filled the speakers. Over the music a voice announced the first competitor.

"Our first entrant is Natalie Whittemore."

Jamil scanned the crowd one more time for the mysterious person. "Oh, no." He groaned. He spotted the *News* reporter Debbie Windsor. Now he knew something was going to go wrong. She was always around when something happened. But it was too late to do anything.

Jamil anxiously stood on his toes to get a better view

of the landing area.

Nat took off down the slope toward the jump.

Everyone watched her adjust her speed and position herself for the perfect jump.

When Nat hit the lip of the jump, she flew into the air and hucked her board up so she could bring a big, clean method into the world. As she did this, her body arced gracefully above the crowd. Her form was perfect.

In those seconds that Nat floated in the air, Jamil's eyes darted to the spot where she would land. He spotted the dark figure lift one of the buckets and hurl it onto the slope. Water splashed across the powder. The mysterious person picked up the other bucket and tossed more water onto the landing area.

Total disaster!

"Nat!" Jamil screamed.

Nat came down hard and landed right in the middle of the puddle. Her board shot out from under her and she flipped down the slope.

"Nasty!" Kevin gasped. He was up on his feet and then sliding on his rear down the slope toward her.

Nat skidded into the fence and didn't move.

The crowd groaned.

Jamil frantically searched the crowd for the dark figure. He had lost sight of the person when Nat fell.

Suddenly, a shadowy figure disappeared into the woods. It looked like the person was on a snowboard. He was riding directly into the woods and away from the slope!

Jamil strapped on his snowboard and rode down to where he spotted the dark rider. Under the floodlights he made out clear snowboard boot tracks. They were a strange-looking tread of diamonds encircling arrows that pointed to a shape that looked like a tongue sticking out.

69

"Wall!" Jamil gasped. Wall's treadmarks! He *had* been wrong! It wasn't Mitch—it was Wall who was causing all the trouble!

Jamil darted into the woods. As he left the light of the slopes, he was glad that there was a full moon. It shone brightly through the bare trees, highlighting the shadows in the dark boarder's tracks.

Surfing trees was difficult during the light of day, but it was nearly impossible at night. Jamil carved through a tight alley between two pine trees.

In his mind he kept repeating to himself, Don't look at the trees. Keep your eyes on the open spaces.

From experience, Jamil knew that if you looked at the trees to avoid them, you usually rode right into them. And that could be disastrous. The last thing he wanted was to get sucked into a tree well. A rider could drown in a tree well, a hole that forms when the snow around the tree collapses inward.

Jamil locked his eyes on the boarder tracks ahead of him and used that line as a guide. He kept his board pointed toward the gaps in the trees, while his body pumped up and down with each quick, tight turn.

"Whoa!" Jamil whispered to himself as his hat got caught on a low-hanging branch. "Too close."

Jamil came to a stop. He couldn't see the tracks. A cloud had moved in front of the moon and blocked its light. As he glanced around, he realized he was far from the resort. There was nothing else to do but push on. He slid sideways through the trees at a snail's pace. He looked up at the sky through the tangle of branches. The moon was still hidden.

He pushed on, avoiding trees and sliding over rocks. His board was being torn to shreds, but Jamil didn't care. He just wanted to nail the person who had tried to break Nat's neck.

Jamil stopped. It was now way too dark to go on. He searched the snow-blanketed forest floor for board tracks. He squatted, hoping to get a better view. He thought he could see the tracks moving off to the left.

He looked up at the sky one more time and saw one bright star shining through the clouds. He made a wish on it and moved on tentatively.

Suddenly, he heard a soft crunching sound. Wall is off his board, Jamil thought. He felt reassured that he hadn't lost him.

"Wall?" Jamil called ahead. There was no response. Once again, the sound of crunching snow echoed through the trees. "Wall?" Jamil called out again. This time he heard a distinctly human grunt. He located the sound as coming from a cluster of trees to his right. Jamil rode slowly in that direction.

CRACK! A loud sound exploded from the direction behind him.

Jamil glanced over his shoulder and didn't see the person come out from the shadows of the tree next to him.

The person held a large tree branch. As Jamil came close, the person swung.

THWOP! The branch whizzed through the air and

hit Jamil across the chest.

Jamil flew backward. His feet were locked into the snowboard bindings, so he couldn't recover his balance. Instead, he tried to sit on his rear, but landed on his back and started to slide.

He was slipping headfirst directly toward a deep tree well!

Within seconds, Jamil was sucking snow. He frantically struggled to push himself out of the well, but that was impossible. He was lying head first on his back in a well at least four feet deep. His feet were still strapped to his board so he couldn't twist and bring his feet under him.

As panic set in, Jamil tried to scream. His voice, however, was muffled by the snow pressed against his face.

It was so cold. So cold.

His head spun as the blood rushed to it. He closed his eyes. He thought he was starting to lose consciousness. He felt himself suddenly rising or floating or something. His face was no longer pressed against the snow. The blood stopped pressing on his forehead.

He began hearing a voice. It was speaking something. It was speaking his name.

"Jamil!"

The voice sounded familiar.

"Jamil!"

Tentatively, he opened his eyes. "Wall!" he gasped. This was the last person he expected to see. Didn't he just try to kill him?

"Relax, it's me," Wall whispered.

"Get away!" Jamil screamed as he tried to drag himself out of Wall's reach. "You just tried to kill me! And you just tried to kill Nat!" Jamil frantically pulled at his bindings to free his feet. He wanted to be ready if Wall attacked him again.

"Not me!" Wall yelled. "Melvin! It's Melvin! He's doing it." Wall pointed to Chip, who flailed helplessly in the tree well he'd just pulled Jamil out of.

Finally the cloud blocking the moon's light passed and the bright light of the full moon swept across Chip's face.

"Melvin?" Jamil said as he sat up.

"When Melvin knocked you into the tree well, I came up behind him," Wall explained, "and gave him a little push."

"Melvin?" Jamil asked. He looked down at Chip in the well. "Your name is Melvin?" Jamil said snidely.

"Chip's his nickname," Wall explained.

"Help! Jamil, really, I'm hurt!" Chip cried.

"Serves you right," Jamil said.

"Whoa," Wall screamed, leaping back and pulling Jamil with him to safety.

The snow in front of them began collapsing right on Chip.

Chip's head popped up out of the snow.

"He'll be all right," Wall said.

Suddenly, the loud grinding of snowmobiles drowned out their conversation. The bright headlights blinded them as the snowmobiles crashed through the woods.

It was the Hoke Valley ski patrol.

"Hey!" Jamil called to them. "Over here!"

As they approached, the patrol leader, Mike Shanahan, asked, "What happened?"

Jamil and Wall pointed down to Chip, half covered in snow.

The patrol quickly pulled Chip out of the tree well.

As soon as Chip was safe, Jamil started firing questions. "First—Wall, what are you doing here?"

Wall shrugged. "I know Melvin, I mean Chip, from Barton Mountain. His dad owns Barton."

"He's the old guy's son?" Jamil said, shocked.

"When I saw him working at Hoke Valley, I sort of figured he was up to something," Wall explained, "but I didn't exactly know what until I saw him tonight and I thought he might really hurt someone. So I kept my mouth shut."

"So he's responsible for everything," Jamil said.

"Except the first sign," Wall added. "That was Mitch."

"Okay," Jamil repeated, "except the first sign." Then, Jamil wheeled around toward Chip.

"So you caused all this trouble just to get Hoke Valley's boarder business?" Jamil asked him disgustedly.

Chip finally had to admit that he'd been busted.

"You could have killed us!" Jamil shouted.

Chip avoided Jamil's eyes. "Things got out of hand, that's for sure. But you should've minded your own business."

"You're out of your mind," Jamil muttered. He turned to Mike Shanahan. "How'd you find us?"

"That reporter from the *News*," Mike explained. "She saw you and Wall take off into the woods and alerted us. She thought you were responsible for the sabotage on the big air." He nodded at Wall.

"Well, thanks for coming," Wall said.

"Yeah," Mike said. "Let's get back." Jamil and Wall climbed on the back of Mike's snowmobile, while Chip rode on the back of the other snowmobile. In minutes they were back at the lodge. The crowd had thinned, but the mariachi band was still performing.

Nat was sitting in a lounge chair with an ice pack on her neck. Kevin sat beside her.

When the snowmobiles pulled to a stop, Jamil and Wall dashed to Nat's side. Mike Shanahan led Chip to the office, where he planned to call the state police.

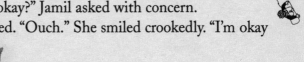

"Are you okay?" Jamil asked with concern.

Nat nodded. "Ouch." She smiled crookedly. "I'm okay

as long as I don't move my head. I sprained my neck."

"Brutal," Wall responded. "Do you need anything?"

"Just a new neck," Nat answered. "And to find out what happened."

Jamil explained how Chip orchestrated the whole thing.

Nat shook her head in disbelief. "Well, thanks to Wall the mystery's solved. We definitely could use your help next time a mind-boggling case comes our way."

Wall shrugged, but a corner of his lip curled up in a shy smile. "The important thing is that you're okay."

"The doctor said she'll be all right," Kevin explained. "She'll be sore for a couple of days, but that's all."

"How about a milk shake?" Jamil asked.

"Not now," Nat replied. "Just tell the band to stop. I've got a horrible headache."

"That's easy," Jamil said as he went outside and spoke to his dad. By the time Jamil got back the band had stopped. "So who won?" he asked.

"Your dad canceled the big air," Kevin explained. "The slope was too dangerous after what Chip did."

"I'll take some hot chocolate now," Nat said.

"Oh, poor baby," Jamil said with fake sympathy. "Do you want me to kiss your boo boo? Would you like a blanky, too?"

"Ha, ha," Nat replied sarcastically.

16

Early the next morning, Jamil padded down the stairs to the kitchen.

His dad was sitting at the breakfast table, drinking coffee and reading the paper. He looked up when Jamil came into the kitchen. "We made the front page."

Jamil glanced over his dad's shoulder and saw the lead article in the paper. The headline read: HOKE VALLEY CATCHES SABOTEUR RED-HANDED.

Jamil glowed with pride over having caught Chip and proved to his dad that boarders aren't always troublemakers.

"I just got a call from the police," Mr. Smith said. "Chip is being charged with assault for what he did last night. If we're lucky, they'll be able to book him for vandalism as well."

"Wow!" Jamil exclaimed. He poured himself a glass of milk and sat across from his dad. "What's going to happen to him?"

"I'm pressing charges," Mr. Smith said firmly. "He almost ruined Hoke Valley's reputation. If he had achieved what he set out to do, he would have really hurt business next year. The word would have been out that Hoke Valley isn't safe."

"And newly renovated Barton Mountain would have picked up all our business." Jamil shook his head in disbelief.

"You got it," Mr. Smith replied. He sipped his coffee.

"I just can't believe Chip would do something like that," Jamil continued. "I mean, he seemed like such a nice guy."

"I know," Mr. Smith said, "and I depended on him."

"I kind of feel for Chip's dad," Jamil added. "He seemed so proud of his son. He thought his son was going to save Barton Mountain. Now what's going to happen between them?"

The two of them sat quietly for a few minutes.

Finally, Mr. Smith broke the silence. "I've got to head to the office. Today is going to be brutal. Besides running the carnival, I'm going to have to deal with the police and the media." He got up, washed out his coffee cup, and put on his jacket.

"Are you going to be able to see me race this afternoon?" Jamil said hopefully.

Mr. Smith shook his head. "I've got to set up for tonight's Italian Festival. We still don't have enough Chianti bottles for the candles."

Jamil looked down at the table, disappointed. His

father said good-bye, but Jamil wouldn't meet his eyes. He just got up and left the room.

On the way out, Jamil muttered, "I wish you'd just take me seriously like you did Chip. Then, maybe you could depend on me instead."

Later that day, Jamil had made it to the final round of the boardercross, while Wall and Kevin got knocked out in the first round. Jamil stood at the starting line with Mitch to his right and Corey Blake to his left. Blake had the fastest time so far on the course.

Jamil looked to both sides of him. He swallowed hard. A nervous shiver rolled down his spine. At that crucial moment Mitch tapped him on the shoulder. Jamil groaned inwardly.

"Uh, Jamil, I just wanted to thank you for explaining things to your dad," Mitch mumbled. "If you hadn't, I wouldn't be able to ride today."

And you wouldn't be bugging me right now, Jamil thought. "No prob. But I guess my dad worked out a plan for you to make up for your bogus stunts by working in the off-season."

Mitch grinned mischievously. "Yeah, summer. But being banned shook me up. I'll keep the pranks off the slopes, at least."

"Great, wonderful," Jamil said, turning away. He tried to focus his attention downslope again and calm his pounding heart.

The announcer was introducing the racers over the

loudspeaker. Jamil stretched his arms and began to crouch in preparation of the starting gun.

"Go, Speed Racer!" Nat yelled from the sidelines.

Jamil looked down the slope to smile at her, but he caught sight of another face instead. It was his dad's.

Mr. Smith gave his son a big thumbs-up. Jamil grinned.

"On your mark!" the announcer began.

A wave of calm flowed through Jamil's limbs.

"Get set!"

A pause that seemed like hours.

BANG! The gun went off.

The boarders shot down the course, shoving and pushing each other aside to get the best position on the first turn. Boardercross was not for the faint of heart. It took steely determination and grit, along with an ability to ride fast across a treacherous course.

Luckily, Jamil flashed ahead of the pack. He flew off the first bonk low and in control. He fought the desire to look over his shoulder and see who was behind him. He knew that would cost him precious tenths of a second. Tenths that could be the difference between winning and losing.

Instead, Jamil hurled down the slope. He kept his board close to the ground and fought off all challenges until the last hundred yards. As he hit the final straight-away, Blake started to gain on him. Jamil made the mistake of allowing his board to catch too much air on a jump. It slowed him down and Blake shot past him.

Jamil crouched even lower. He was determined to make up the lost time. As the two shredders approached the finish line, Blake was only inches ahead of Jamil.

But Jamil was picking up speed while Blake was losing it. Just as they crossed, Jamil nosed out Blake for the win!

Jamil flung his arms high in the air as the crowd surged toward him. Everyone around him congratulated him and slapped him on the back. Through the crowd, Jamil spotted Blake sitting in the snow on the side of the hill. Then he saw his dad coming down the slope, jumping up and down and screaming for joy.

Bertle—a wide turn with extreme body lean, named after famous '70s surfer Larry Bertlemann

board—a snowboard

boardhead—a snowboarder

boardercross—a downhill race between five or six competitors

bone it out—to straighten a leg while jumping

bonk—mogul (bump in the snow)

carve—using the edge of the snowboard to turn

catch air—to jump

edge—the metal strip on the bottom sides of a board

Eurocarve—a wide turn with extreme body lean done by shredders who never heard of Larry (see Bertle)

facial—to slam your face into the powder

fakie—riding backward

fall line—the line a ball would take rolling down a slope

flat bowl—a shallow, curved section on a slope

goofy—right foot forward stance

halfpipe—a snow-filled gully in which freestyle snowboarders perform aerial maneuvers, much like skateboards on a ramp

hardpack—firm, fast snow, almost icy

heelside—the edge of the board closest to the rider's heels

huck—to come off a bump and take air

indy three—the back hand grabs the toe edge between the toes while making a 360-degree turn in the air

knuckledragger—primordial snowboarders

method—a hand grabs the heel edge between the heels and the front hand and pulls the board up behind as high as the head

nose—the front of the board

ollie—a way of getting airborne on a flat surface by lifting front end of board and pushing off back end

powder—snow that is deep, light, and dry

regular—left foot forward stance

riding—snowboarding

shred—to ride fast and stylishly

shredder—a snowboarder

sidecut—the curve in the side of a board

swag—the free merchandise board manufacturers give out

swany—performing a method with the grace of a swan

tail—the back of the board

tip—the front of the board

toe grab—when boarder grabs toeside of board on a jump

toeside—the edge of the board closest to the rider's toes

tree well—a hole in the snow surrounding a tree

tweak—pulling the board forward or behind while in the air

If you're looking for suspense on the slopes,
harrowing adventure on the half pipe, or
mystery on the trails, look no further!

#1 Deep Powder, Deep Trouble

Jamil must nab a mysterious rogue rider, or snowboarding
at Hoke Valley will be banned forever.

#2 Crossed Tracks

Who's sabotaging the Bear Claw Mountain bike course?
Nat's determined to find out!

#3 Rocked Out: A Summer
X Games Special

Kevin and Wall are volunteers at the Summer X Games
and become embroiled in a sport-climbing mystery.

#4 Half Pipe Rip-off

Wall needs to track down the graffiti fiend who's framing
him for vandalism.

Get Amped for the X Games Xtreme Mysteries

Shred It Up This Spring!

Available Now

X Games Xtreme Mysteries #1
Deep Powder, Deep Trouble
ISBN 0-7868-1284-2

X Games Xtreme Mysteries #2
Crossed Tracks
ISBN 0-7868-1281-8

Coming in June

X Games Xtreme Mysteries #3
Rocked Out: A Summer X Games
Special
ISBN 0-7868-1283-4

X Games Xtreme Mysteries #4
Half Pipe Rip-Off
ISBN 0-7868-1282-6

Every single book is jammed to the max with Xtras:

- full-color photo insert featuring action shots of a champion X Games athlete, his/her tips on safety, and a complete bio
- exclusive special offers
- player stats
- the X Games broadcast schedule
- plus much more

Disney's Daily BLAST ^{SM}

THE ONLINE SERVICE FOR KIDS

TRY IT FREE TODAY!

- **PLAY** fast paced games against live opponents.

- **SOLVE** online mysteries & steer the action in interactive stories.

- **DESIGN** party activities in your own online print studio.

- **SEND & RECEIVE** exciting, animated e-mail.

AND MUCH, MUCH MORE!

FOR A ONE MONTH FREE TRIAL,

go to **www.disneyblast.com/xtreme**

or skip the download and get your FREE CD-ROM by calling toll-free

1 (888) 594-BLAST today!